Happily Ever After Stories

Tales of Love and Friendship

New York

TABLE OF CONTENTS

Ariel and the Sea-Horse Race

King Triton, ruler of all the oceans, stormed into the palace courtyard. "Ariel!" he bellowed, summoning his daughter.

The young mermaid was nearby, riding her sea horse, Stormy. "Uh-oh," Ariel said worriedly. "He sounds angry." She turned Stormy around, and they went to the courtyard.

King Triton glared at Ariel. "How could you sign up for the annual Sea-Horse Race?" he demanded. "It's a dangerous competition—for mermen! No mermaid has ever competed."

Ariel raised her chin defiantly. "Mermaids ride sea horses, too, Daddy," she said. "And Stormy may be small, but he's fast. I know we can win that race if you'll let us enter."

"Absolutely not!" King Triton shouted.

"But, Daddy . . ." Ariel pleaded.

"No, Ariel. I forbid you to enter the race!" he said sternly.

Ariel and Stormy slowly made their way out of the courtyard— the mermaid knew her father would never change his mind.

Ariel moped around the racecourse all week long. Her best friend, Flounder, tried to cheer her up.

"The race trophy isn't really that great," said Flounder. "I know what would make you happy—looking for some snarfblatts or dinglehoppers."

But for once, Ariel didn't want to look for human objects that had fallen into the sea. She only had one thing on her mind: the race.

"It just isn't fair!" she exclaimed. "I know I could win!"

"Yes," agreed Flounder. "If only you were a merman. Then your father would let you enter the race."

"That's it!" cried Ariel. "I'll be a merman—Arrol, the merman! Flounder, you're a genius!"

8

Ariel zipped around the palace, looking for a racing uniform and helmet. As she turned a corner, she swam straight into her father's adviser, Sebastian the crab.

"Teenagers," Sebastian muttered, "always in a hurry."

"Sorry," Ariel said. "I guess I just had racing on my mind."

"You and your father both," the crab said as he adjusted his shell. "He keeps going to the closet to look at his old racing uniform. You know, he was your age when he entered his first competition."

Ariel was surprised. King Triton had never told her that he used to race.

"Thanks, Sebastian!" said Ariel. Now she knew where to find a racing uniform!

On the morning of the competition, Ariel went to the starting line with Stormy. She was disguised in her father's racing gear with her hair hidden under a helmet. No one had noticed her yet.

King Triton raised his trident. A spark shot out of it, and the sea horses took off. The racers steered them through the water at breakneck speed. When they reached the coral reef, many of the fastest and most powerful sea horses could not fit through

the small openings and had to swim around the coral reef.

But Stormy was small and Ariel was brave, so they swam through the reef. Before long, they had taken the lead.

Ariel shouted with joy as her sea horse whipped around the next turn. But this time he was *too* fast! Ariel's helmet hit the coral and popped off. Her long red hair streamed out behind her as they headed into a dark cavern.

One racer, Carpa, saw Ariel's red hair from behind. "A mermaid!" he cried in disbelief. He raced as quickly as he could, trying to overtake her.

It was pitch black in the cavern, but Ariel and Stormy knew the way. They had been there many times before to search for treasure.

Suddenly, Ariel and Stormy heard someone behind them. It was Carpa. He was closing in on them!

Stormy swam out of the cavern at record speed. He headed for the last part of the racecourse: the seaweed hurdles.

Ariel and Stormy swam over and under the seaweed hurdles. Now all of Atlantica could see them. The crowd gasped as the princess passed by with Carpa right next to her. King Triton rose from the royal box, a look of utter surprise on his face.

"Come on, Stormy!" Ariel urged. With one last burst of speed, the sea horse raced across the finish line—he and Ariel won!

"Hooray!" the crowd roared. Even Carpa clapped—the mermaid had beat him fair and square.

Ariel smiled and waved. Then she saw her father. "I'm sorry, Daddy—" she began.

"No, Ariel, *I'm* sorry," he interrupted. "I had forgotten how much fun racing is. I was just worried about you. Can you ever forgive me?"

Ariel nodded and kissed his cheek. Then, King Triton proudly handed his daughter the trophy.

Everyone cheered, but the king was the most enthusiastic of all.

Belle's Tea Party

*B*elle looked out the window sadly. It had been raining for six straight days, and she felt cooped up. She hadn't taken a walk or visited the stables in nearly a week. "Will the rain ever stop?" she wondered.

Chip the little teacup was wondering the same thing. He had already played all the games he could think of. Now he just wished he could go outside. Since he was so little, he didn't have a job like the other enchanted objects.

But the rest of the enchanted objects had finished their work. The castle was spotless.

Lumiere the candelabrum wandered into the dining room. He noticed how bored Chip and Belle looked and began to sing a song in French.

Then Cogsworth the clock rounded up some napkins, spoons, and bowls, and led them in a dance. "That's it!" he cried as they whirled around the table.

"Hooray!" Chip yelled when the song was over.

"That was wonderful!" Belle cried. "Will you do another song?"

Lumiere frowned. "Actually, we need to go check on the master," he said.

"Yes," Cogsworth agreed. "He might need something." He and Lumiere hopped off the table and went to the Beast's study.

"Now what will we do, Belle?" Chip asked.

Belle looked over at the teacup and smiled. "I'm not sure, Chip," she said. "I'll try to think of something."

Just then, Chip's mother, Mrs. Potts the teapot, entered the room. She knew just what would cheer up Belle and Chip.

"Let's have a tea party," she suggested. "Belle, why don't you change into your prettiest party dress? And Chip, I have a special job for you."

The little teacup smiled excitedly, and Belle raced upstairs to change.

"We're going to have a tea party!" Belle exclaimed when she reached her room.

"Oh, that's lovely, dear!" the Wardrobe replied. "You'll need something bright and pretty to wear." She opened one door and looked inside. Belle reached for a navy dress. "No, no, no!" the Wardrobe cried. "That's too dark for a tea party."

The Wardrobe rummaged around a little more and found a yellow hat. "You simply must wear this," she said.

"It's beautiful!" Belle cried. Then she noticed that the Wardrobe was holding a yellow-and-gold dress and matching gloves. "Oh, you've outdone yourself," she said.

The Wardrobe smiled proudly.

After Belle had changed, she looked in the mirror and twirled around. It was such fun to dress up!

"You'll be the belle of the ball . . . er, tea party," the Wardrobe said with a giggle.

Meanwhile, Lumiere and Cogsworth returned to the dining room. The Beast had been taking a nap, so they hadn't needed to do anything for him.

Once the clock and candelabrum heard about the tea party, they started getting the dining room ready. They put a vase filled with blue flowers on the table. Then the spoons, dishes, and napkins jumped into place. Now all they needed was the food.

Before long, Mrs. Potts and Chip brought in some tiny sandwiches and some pastries with frosting.

"Ooh la la!" Lumiere cried. "This will be a wonderful tea party. I think we are almost ready."

"Ahem," Cogsworth said. "Chip, would you please place this card at the head of the table?" He gave Chip a card with Belle's name on it. "That way she'll know where to sit."

Chip put the card in place. Mrs. Potts smiled at her son. "Now you take your place, too," she said. The little teacup hopped onto a saucer excitedly. It was his first tea party, and he couldn't wait for it to begin.

23

"Everything is so beautiful!" Belle exclaimed as she walked into the dining room.

"But wait," said Mrs. Potts. "We can't forget the most important part of the tea party . . . the tea!"

Mrs. Potts tipped herself over and poured some tea into Chip. Then Belle picked up Chip and took a sip.

The little teacup beamed. At last, he had an important job.

"This is a lovely tea party," Belle said. "I'm so glad I have good friends like you."

"Me, too," Chip said.

Everyone smiled. Maybe rainy days weren't so bad after all.

Walt Disney's Cinderella

My Perfect Wedding

Cinderella's dreams were coming true at last! With the help of her mouse friends, she had managed to race down the stairs just in time to let the Grand Duke place a glass slipper on her foot. That proved she was the girl that the Prince had met and fallen in love with at the royal ball.

Now she and the Prince were going to be married, and their brand-new life together would soon begin. But first, there was a wedding to plan, and Cinderella didn't have the faintest idea where to begin.

Prudence, who ran the castle household for the King, was happy to take charge. She sat with Cinderella and read off a long list of things that needed to be done for the wedding.

"Excuse me," Cinderella said as soon as Prudence had paused for a moment, "but couldn't the Prince and I just have a simple wedding?"

Prudence frowned. "Cinderella, now that you are going to be a princess you need to start thinking like one. This should be the grandest wedding the kingdom has ever seen!"

29

Later on, the royal dressmaker arrived with several wedding gowns. The first gown Cinderella tried on was covered with bows and sashes, and had a huge skirt. "The guests will mistake me for a present!" she cried.

"You look just like a princess!" Prudence said.

But Cinderella thought the dress was too fussy. "Do you think you could design something plainer?" she asked.

"'Plain' and 'princess' do not go together!" Prudence said.

The next day, Prudence and Cinderella visited the royal florist. He presented them with a bouquet of roses that was so big, it looked more like a bush.

"Do you have something a bit smaller?" Cinderella asked.

"It's perfect," Prudence said. "You just have to know how to carry it." She grabbed the flowers—and a bee flew out. *Bzzz, bzzz!* Prudence screamed, and the bee stung her. Then she screamed even louder!

That afternoon, the mice found Cinderella all by herself in the garden. "Where's bossy lady?" asked Gus.

"Poor Prudence," replied Cinderella. "She got quite a nasty bee sting. The royal physician says she has to stay in bed for the rest of the day."

"But what about the wedding plans?" Jaq asked.

"I'll just have to take care of them myself!" Cinderella declared. "Look at the size of this list! What do you think I should do first?"

"Who's-a comin', Cinderelly?" wondered Jaq.

"The guest list! Good idea, Jaq. Let's see. Well, of course, all of you are invited," Cinderella replied. "And my Fairy Godmother, too . . . I wish she were here right now."

Almost as fast as Cinderella made her wish, the Fairy Godmother appeared!

"I just love weddings," the Fairy Godmother said. "And I'm sure everything you've picked out is wonderful!"

Cinderella admitted she hadn't started planning.

"When is the wedding, dear?" asked the Fairy Godmother.

Gus counted on his fingers. "Tomorrow!" he announced.

"Oh, my goodness, child!" cried the Fairy Godmother. "We'd better get started!"

"Lots to do!" Jaq added. He and Gus showed Prudence's list to the Fairy Godmother.

"We'll plan an absolutely magical wedding for you, dear!" the Fairy Godmother gushed. "Now, let's begin with the dress." She waved her wand, and Cinderella was instantly adorned in an elegant white gown. But the Fairy Godmother had forgotten something.

"It's beautiful," Cinderella said. "But don't you think it needs a veil?"

The Fairy Godmother wasn't listening, though. She had already moved on to the next item. "Invitations!" she declared. In the blink of an eye, thousands of lovely cards sat in stacks around the room.

"Now we shall prepare the feast and make the cake!" the Fairy Godmother announced. Cinderella changed back into her blue dress and followed the Fairy Godmother to the royal kitchen.

Meanwhile, three of the mice lifted some scissors and cut a small piece of fabric from underneath Cinderella's wedding gown. Then they threaded needles, pulled out a box of tiny pearls, and began to make a veil.

The rest of the mice each took a stack of cards to deliver. They didn't get very far before their plans were spoiled by Pom-Pom, the castle cat!

"Whew! Close-a call!" Jaq cried as he and Gus raced to the kitchen, where Cinderella was with the Fairy Godmother.

"And now for the best part!" the Fairy Godmother exclaimed. With one grand sweep of her wand, she created the biggest, fanciest cake Cinderella had ever seen.

"What do you think?" the Fairy Godmother asked.

"Um . . . Prudence will love it," Cinderella said, trying to hide her disappointment. "And speaking of Prudence, I really should go see how she's feeling."

"Poor child," the Fairy Godmother said after Cinderella had left. "I think all these wedding plans are too much for her."

Jaq and Gus tugged at the Fairy Godmother's sleeve. "Cinderelly like smaller things," Jaq told her. Gus pointed proudly to himself. "Like mice!"

All at once, the Fairy Godmother understood why Cinderella hadn't been thrilled.

The Fairy Godmother went to Cinderella's room a little later. "I'm afraid I may have gotten a bit carried away, my dear," she confessed. "Now tell me, what would the wedding of your dreams be like?"

After listening to Cinderella, the Fairy Godmother began to perform her magic. With a wave of her wand, the veil was finished. Then the invitations were sent to a smaller group of people.

"Now let's cut that cake down to size," the Fairy Godmother said, with a twinkle in her eye.

As they walked in to the kitchen, Cinderella turned to the mice. "Thank you, my little friends," she said gratefully.

"Anything for you Cinderelly!" Jaq said.

"Bibbidi-Bobbidi-Boo!" the Fairy Godmother cried as she pointed at the cake. It shrank and shrank until it was the size of a normal wedding cake.

The next day, Cinderella got ready for her wedding. She wore a simple white gown, veil, and gloves. She carried a bouquet of garden roses that the mice had gathered for her. It was just as she had dreamed.

But as the King was about to escort her down the aisle, Cinderella looked down and gave a little cry of surprise. She wasn't wearing any shoes! What would she do? She looked at the mice then down at her feet again.

The Fairy Godmother followed the bride's gaze. "Good heavens, child!" she exclaimed. "You can't get married in your bare feet!" She waved her wand, and suddenly Cinderella was wearing glass slippers!

After the ceremony, there was a joyful party. It wasn't the kingdom's grandest celebration, but it was the most special. Even Prudence was pleased.

"How ever did you manage all of this?" the Prince asked Cinderella.

The princess smiled and said, "With friends by your side, anything is possible!"

Disney's Aladdin

One True Love

Aladdin, Princess Jasmine, and Jasmine's tiger, Rajah, were relaxing in the palace courtyard when they heard a familiar voice.

"I'm *baaack*!" the Genie yelled. "How's my favorite couple?"

"We've missed you," Jasmine said. "How was your trip around the world?"

"Fabulous!" the Genie replied. "I saw the pyramids in Egypt, went skiing in Sweden, and worked on my tan in the Caribbean. I'm a nice shade of blue, don't you think?"

A spark flew from the Genie's finger, and soon Aladdin and
Jasmine were surrounded by gifts from every country the Genie
had visited! He'd brought a special surprise for Aladdin: a
kangaroo from Australia!

"Whoa, little guy," Aladdin said as the kangaroo bounced
over his foot. But the animal didn't stop—it kept hopping until it
leaped over the palace wall. "Hey, hold on!" Aladdin yelled. He
turned to Jasmine. "I'd better go catch it!"

"Be careful!" the Genie yelled as Aladdin took off. "Kangaroos
know how to box!"

"Oh, Genie, it's good to have you back in Agrabah," said Jasmine. Then she noticed that he looked a little sad. "What's the matter?" she asked. "You seem blue."

"I've always been blue," he said with a grin. Then he got serious. "All that traveling was great, but I was a bit lonely," he said. "I wish I could find another genie to share my life with."

Jasmine put her hand on the Genie's shoulder. "I know how you feel," she said. "I went through a lot of suitors before I found my one true love."

The princess began to tell the Genie her story. "I told my father that I wanted to marry for love," Jasmine explained. "But the law said that I had to marry a prince. No matter what I said, my father wouldn't listen to me. He summoned every suitor he could find to come and court me."

"Sounds like you were pretty popular," the Genie commented.

"Popular? Yes," Jasmine replied. "Happy? No!"

"At first, I tried to make the best of the situation," Jasmine said. "I knew my father was counting on me. He had the seamstresses make brand-new outfits for me. It was fun in the beginning, trying on one beautiful outfit after another."

"You must have looked gorgeous, dahling!" interrupted the Genie.

"And then, of course, there were the jewels. It all seemed too good to be true . . . till I met the suitors," Jasmine said with a sigh. "Then I wasn't so excited."

"First there was Prince Achoo, or at least that's what I called him," Jasmine continued.

"'Princess Jasmine,' he said. '*A-a-a-choo*! It's so—*achoo!*—nice to meet you.'"

The Genie laughed. "Was he allergic to you?" he asked.

"Not me," said Jasmine. "Just my perfume, the throne room, and everything in the palace. I couldn't take it, so I sent him packing. He sneezed his way out the door."

"As the days passed, each suitor seemed worse than the one before," Jasmine said. "Next was the prince I called Prince Macho.

"'The princess I marry will do all the cooking and cleaning, and whatever other housework is needed,' he told me. I was shocked. 'You want me to wait on you hand and foot?' I asked.

"'It is important for me to relax,' Prince Macho said.

"'Oh, really?' I said. 'It's important to me that my husband isn't living in the Stone Age!'

"He stormed off—I was happy that he left."

"Wow, he sounds terrible," the Genie said. "I'm glad you got rid of him!"

"Next was Prince Wishy-Washy," said Jasmine. "I asked him what he liked to do.

"'Whatever you like to do, Princess,' he replied."

"Sounds like a barrel of laughs," the Genie said.

Jasmine smiled. "I asked him what he liked to eat.

"'Whatever you eat, Princess,' he replied. So I decided to have a little fun. I told him we were having roasted ant pitas with rat hummus for lunch. He turned green and left the room."

"Princess, I'm shocked," the Genie said, laughing.

She smiled at him impishly. "Well, at least he made up his mind about something. I was very happy with his decision!"

"Just when I had almost lost hope, I met Aladdin," Jasmine said. "He rescued me from an angry street vendor after I took an apple for a hungry child. Then, with your help, Genie, he turned himself into a prince and came to my balcony."

"Yeah, Al never looked better," the Genie said.

"But it wasn't how he looked, Genie. It was what he said. He told me that he understood I wasn't a prize to be won, and that I should be able to decide who I wanted to marry. Then he took me on the most wonderful ride on the Magic Carpet. And true love blossomed."

Jasmine smiled happily, then looked over at the Genie.
He was bawling like a baby! "Genie? Genie! What's wrong?"
the princess asked.

"That was the sweetest story I've ever heard!" the Genie
said between sobs.

Jasmine laughed and became a
bit embarrassed. "Genie,
you can find the same
happiness that Aladdin
and I share. I just know
your special genie is
out there!"

"Really?" asked
the Genie.

"Yes, really,"
Jasmine replied.

Just then, Aladdin showed up with the kangaroo. "You were right, Genie. That kangaroo has a strong right punch," he said, holding his arm.

"No time to talk, Al," said the Genie, rushing past. "I've got a genie to find—and not a thing to wear!"

"What's with him?" Aladdin asked Jasmine.

"He wants to have what we have," the princess replied with a smile. "True love."

Within minutes, the Genie reappeared. He did a quick fashion show for Jasmine and Aladdin. "Do I go for the handsome banker look? Or maybe the preppy golfer thing? Or what about a surfer dude with 'tude? Which one works best?" the Genie asked.

56

"You want someone to like you for who you are on the inside," Jasmine advised. "Just be yourself."

"Myself?" the Genie said. "You mean like who I really am in my heart, not the people I change myself into?"

"Exactly," Jasmine replied.

"I wonder who that is?" the Genie said.

"C'mon, Genie," Aladdin said. "You're a great guy—funny, smart, helpful, and kind. You're a wonderful friend, and some lucky lady genie is going to realize that. Like Jasmine said, just be yourself."

A lightbulb went on above the Genie's head. He looked at Jasmine and Aladdin. "Presto-change-o!" he said, and the surfer clothes vanished. "How do you like my new . . . er . . . old look?"

"It's perfect," Jasmine said warmly.

"Thanks," the Genie said and took off.

"How about a ride on the Magic Carpet?" Aladdin asked Jasmine tenderly.

"I'd love it," replied Jasmine. "I was just telling the Genie about our *first* carpet ride."

As Jasmine and Aladdin flew above Agrabah, the princess snuggled close to her husband.

After a while, a mountaintop came into view. Suddenly Jasmine spotted a blanket and food. "Our own private picnic!" she exclaimed.

"Do you like it?" Aladdin asked.

"Like it? I love it. Oh, Aladdin! I'm so lucky to have you!" Jasmine cried.

Aladdin shook his head. "No, *I'm* the lucky one."

They smiled at each other. Soon the Magic Carpet came to a stop. Aladdin offered Jasmine his hand and led her over to the picnic basket.

As they enjoyed their sunset picnic, Jasmine thought again about all her annoying suitors. Because of them, she really appreciated the love that she had finally found with Aladdin. And she knew the Genie would find his own true love, too.

Walt Disney's
Sleeping Beauty
Ready, Set, Throw!

Briar Rose swept a pile of dust and crumbs out the door. "I think I'll go for a walk in the woods," she told her aunts. "It's such a beautiful day."

"That sounds nice, dear," said her aunt Flora.

"Bring back some pecans, and I'll make a pie," Aunt Fauna called.

"Don't be too long," Aunt Merryweather added.

After Briar Rose had found a basket for the nuts, she waved to her aunts and started toward the woods.

Soon she reached a small stream. A snail family clung to a leafy twig that was floating in the water. "The wind must have blown your branch into the stream," Briar Rose said. "Here, let me help."

She picked up the branch and set it on the grass. "Hurry home," she told the snails. Then she giggled. "Well, I know snails don't hurry, so maybe I should just say have a safe journey."

As Briar Rose continued on, something furry raced by. It was two squirrels! They scampered across a log that had fallen over the stream, climbed up a tree, and disappeared into a hollow. Soon they ran down the tree and hurried toward a pile of pecans.

Briar Rose began to gather nuts and noticed that the squirrels were collecting them, too. When she saw them running back and forth from the nut pile to the tree, she realized they were storing food for the winter.

"Oh, my," she told them. "It's going to take you all day. I wonder if I can help."

Briar Rose looked at the tree. It wasn't that far away. She picked up a nut and threw it at the hollow. *Plop!* It landed in front of the tree. "Hmm," she said, "I bet I can do better." She took aim and threw again. This time, the nut sailed right into the hollow!

Surprised and pleased, she tossed another nut. It went in, too! Briar Rose clapped her hands excitedly. Then she counted out five more pecans. Two missed, but three went in!

"This is fun!" she exclaimed. "And the more nuts that go in, the easier it'll be for the squirrels!"

Just then, Briar Rose's aunt Flora walked over. "You've been gone quite a while, dear."

"Sorry," Briar Rose replied. "I was playing a game and lost track of time."

"What kind of game?" asked Flora.

"I'm trying to toss pecans into that hollow," Briar Rose said, pointing to the tree. "It's fun, plus it helps the squirrels." She handed a nut to her aunt. "Why don't you give it a try?"

Flora threw the pecan quickly. It flew past the tree. "I'm not very good at this," she said with a sigh.

"Don't give up, Aunt Flora," Briar Rose said. "Try again."

Flora took a pecan, aimed, and then threw more gently. It went in!

"Good for you!" exclaimed Briar Rose.

A few minutes later, Merryweather found them. "Oh, there you are!" she exclaimed. "I was starting to worry." She paused. "What are you two doing?"

"We're helping the squirrels," Briar Rose replied.

"Come and play!" Flora added.

Merryweather picked up a nut. "Here goes," she said.

She threw slowly. *Splash!* The nut fell into the stream. Merryweather was determined, though. She kept throwing pecans. One hit a squirrel on the head. It giggled, but Merryweather frowned. "I'll never get it," she said.

"Don't give up," Briar Rose said encouragingly. Flora handed Merryweather five more pecans.

Merryweather picked one up, closed one eye, and took aim. Then she threw as hard as she could. This time, the nut sailed right into the tree hollow!

"Hooray!" Flora and Briar Rose cried.

Just then, Fauna strolled over to the group. "Goodness," she said. "I couldn't imagine what was keeping everyone."

"We're playing a game," Merryweather explained. "Join us."

"It's great fun!" Flora added.

"That's okay," Fauna said as she sat down on a log. "I'll just watch for a while."

The others went back to their game. This time, Briar Rose got all five pecans into the hole. Flora got four in, and Merryweather got three.

"You're both doing so much better," Briar Rose said, complimenting them.

Flora and Merryweather clapped and cheered.

Fauna couldn't stand it any longer. "I think I will play after all," she said. She grabbed a pecan and threw it as hard as she could. The nut zoomed over the stream. Birds flew out of its way as it bounced off a branch, thumped against the ground, then went right into the hollow. The others cheered.

"That was fun!" Fauna exclaimed, jumping up and down. "I want to try again!"

"It's my turn," Flora objected.

But Fauna didn't move. She picked up her green skirt and got down on one knee. She looked right, then left, then threw it.

Again the nut bounced, thumped, and landed in the hole.
"Yes!" Fauna cried. "My trick shot worked!"

"*Trick* shot? It was more like a *lucky* shot," Flora grumbled.

Fauna reached over and stole a pecan from Flora's pile.

"Those are mine!" complained Flora. "And you're in my way."

"Oh, sorry," said Fauna. She stepped aside and bumped into
Merryweather.

"Now you spoiled my shot!" Merryweather complained as the
pecan she'd been about to throw fell to the ground.

"I didn't do it on purpose," Fauna protested.

"Yes, you did," Flora insisted.

Briar Rose watched her aunts in dismay. They had been having so much fun, and now suddenly everyone was angry. What should she do?

"We were helping the squirrels and having a good time," Briar Rose reminded her aunts. "Remember?"

Her aunts just scowled.

"Everyone has different talents. Some of you are better at throwing than others. But you all tried your best. That is what's important," Briar Rose said.

"Briar Rose is right," Merryweather said. "I'm sorry, Fauna. I was jealous of you for that fancy shot."

"I was, too," admitted Flora. "I'm sorry."

"Well, I shouldn't have bragged. And I shouldn't have gotten in your way," said Fauna.

Everyone went to work, picking up the rest of the pecans. Briar Rose and her aunts filled their baskets and put the rest of the pecans into the hollow of the tree.

Then they went back to the cottage.

Merryweather had enough pecans to bake two pies.

Once the pies were in the oven, Flora asked Fauna how she had made that first shot.

"It's easy," Fauna said, jumping up. "I'll show you." She grabbed an egg and started to wind up.

"No!" everyone shouted at the same time, ducking for cover.

"Let's save it for another game," Briar Rose said with a big smile.

Walt Disney's
Snow White
and the Seven Dwarfs
The Little Brown Bear

Snow White walked toward the forest with a basket. She was looking for the sweetest blackberries, boysenberries, and raspberries she could find. She planned to mix them together and bake one of the Dwarfs' favorite desserts— jumble berry pie!

Snow White's woodland friends followed her along the trail. She crossed a winding stream and climbed up a small cliff.

"Why, look at all the berries!" Snow White exclaimed. The bunnies hopped to a nearby bush and happily nibbled on the juicy fruit.

Snow White began to fill her basket. "These are the biggest blackberries I've ever seen," she said. "The pie will be delicious!"

When Snow White's basket was almost full, she heard a strange noise. "I think someone is in trouble," she said.

She and her rabbit friends followed the sound to a hollow log in the middle of a small clearing.

Snow White peeked inside the fallen tree. A brown bear cub was trapped inside!

"Oh, you poor little fellow!" cried Snow White.

The cub whimpered.

"Don't worry," said the princess. "We'll find a way to get you out."

Snow White and the bunnies looked for a way to free the bear cub. The little rabbits began pushing him out of the log, but they were too small.

Snow White reached into the log and tried to pull the cub out, but she couldn't get to him.

"I think we need some help, don't you?" she asked the three little rabbits. They looked at each other, then twitched their noses at her.

"Run to the meadow as quickly as you can and bring the other animals back here," Snow White said. "Please hurry!"

The rabbits nodded their heads and scurried away.

When the bunnies reached the meadow, they told a bird about the little bear cub.

"Tweet! Tweet!" the bird cried. It flew as quickly as it could to tell the other birds, who flew through the forest and told the deer. Next, the message went to the squirrels.

The squirrels ran to share the news with the raccoons, who let the beavers and the moles know. Soon a whole group of animals were making their way toward the bear.

Meanwhile, back in the clearing, Snow White tried to comfort the little cub. "Once when I was a little girl, I got stuck in a tree," she told him. "I climbed all the way to the top, but I couldn't figure out how to get down."

The little bear stopped crying and listened to Snow White's soothing voice.

"But then a kindly farmer came along and helped me get down. So, I know just how you feel," she finished.

The cub peered up at Snow White, and she gently patted his head.

Suddenly, the leaves rustled, birds twittered, and hooves sounded on the ground. Snow White's woodland friends had just arrived.

"Oh, little bear, a lot of my friends have come to help!" Snow White cried. "We'll have you out of there soon."

Snow White and her animal friends gathered around the log. "Can anyone think of a way to set him free?" asked the princess.

Raccoons and squirrels scurried inside the fallen tree to measure its width. The raccoons climbed into one end of the log and pushed the cub, while the squirrels climbed into the other end and pulled him. The moles and the chipmunks even tried to push the log. But they couldn't budge the little bear.

Then the deer stepped forward. They used their large antlers to tip one end of the log up so the bear could slide out. But he was still stuck.

The animals began to get discouraged.

"We can't give up yet!" Snow White cried.

The bird flew to the log and pointed to a small hole at the top. Then he began to peck at it.

After a while, the beavers caught on and began to chew on the log.

The hole grew bigger and bigger as the animals worked together.

"They're making the hole large enough for the little cub to climb out of!" Snow White said excitedly.

Soon the hole was large enough for a beaver to fit through. The beavers chewed faster and faster. Finally, they were done!

Now even a bear cub could fit through the hole.

"Little bear," Snow White called, "it's all right. You can come out now!"

The animals in the clearing watched silently. Nervously, Snow White clasped her hands.

The log rocked back and forth, and Snow White heard a faint rustling sound.

The bear cub's head popped out of the hole, and he looked around at all the animals who had helped him.

Snow White and her friends cheered.

The bear cub wriggled out of the log. He was free!

Snow White gave the little bear a warm hug. "Are you hungry?" she asked.

The bear cub looked at her with interest.

She picked up the basket of ripe berries from the edge of the clearing and set it down near the little bear. He sniffed hungrily.

"Would you like some—" Snow White began. The bear cub ran to the basket and began eating. "—berries?" Snow White finished.

She began to laugh. The bear just kept eating and eating! He seemed to be just fine after his adventure inside the log.

"My, you *are* hungry," said Snow White.

The bear cub looked up from the basket. His face and paws were covered in berry juice.

"I think I'll need to pick some more berries for the Dwarfs' pie!" Snow White exclaimed.

Her animal friends laughed.

The little cub giggled. He was happy to be free and to have made so many new friends.

A Special Song

"May I have your attention, please?" Sebastian called.

The crab tapped his baton on the podium to begin the rehearsal. King Triton's birthday was in a couple of days, and the court musicians were planning a special performance. Triton's daughter, Ariel, would sing while the orchestra played a brand-new tune. Sebastian wanted the concert to be spectacular, but they still had a lot of work to do.

The crab raised his baton, and the musicians began to play. Beautiful music filled the sea, until—*clang!*

"Who did that?" Sebastian demanded.

"Um . . . I did," said a timid voice.

"Not again, Coral!" cried Sebastian.

"Sorry," the young mermaid replied, her cheeks red with embarrassment.

98

"Coral," said the conductor sternly, "the best way to play the cymbals is to hold on to them!"

"Yes, sir," Coral answered.

"Now, if there are no more interruptions," Sebastian said grumpily, "let's continue."

The rehearsal went from bad to worse. Coral kept missing her cues. She dropped her cymbal a second time. *Clang!* Then she tripped and landed on top of the kettledrum.

As Ariel watched, Sebastian threw down his baton. "Rehearsal is over!" the crab yelled and stormed off.

Ariel helped Coral up. "Don't mind Sebastian," she said reassuringly. "He just wants everything to be perfect."

Coral bit her lip. "I might as well quit the orchestra," she said sadly. "I'll never be able to get this song right—let alone perfect."

"Don't worry about it," Ariel said. "The only thing I'm perfect at is making Sebastian mad! You should have seen his face the last time I went to the surface. His eyes bulged right out of his head!"

"You've been to the surface?" Coral asked, amazed. Her face lit up with excitement. "Wow! You must be the bravest mermaid ever!"

Ariel laughed. "I don't know about brave," she said. "It's just something I like to do. I'm sure you have a hobby, right?"

"I don't know," said Coral. "I have nine brothers and sisters, so I'm never really alone."

"I know what you mean," Ariel admitted. "I have a lot of sisters myself. But I have a special place where I keep my collection of treasures. Would you like to see it?"

"I'd love to!" Coral exclaimed.

The two mermaids swam to Ariel's grotto. "Make yourself at home," Ariel said to Coral when they arrived. Flounder the fish was there. He waved a fin at them.

Coral swam around the cavern, examining jewelry and shiny trinkets. "Where did you find all of this?" she asked Ariel as she put on a strand of pearls.

"I found some of it at the bottom of the ocean," said Ariel.

"And in sunken ships," Flounder added.

"You've been inside a sunken ship?" Coral said with a gasp. "Weren't you scared?"

"Of course not. Were you, Flounder?" Ariel teased.

"Nothing to it!" the fish fibbed.

"So what are we waiting for?" Ariel asked. "Let's go!"

Coral and Flounder trailed behind Ariel as she swam. Soon they arrived at a ship that had sunk to the ocean floor.

"Come on!" Ariel urged, disappearing through a large porthole. "Let's see what's inside!"

"She wants us to go in there?" Coral exclaimed.

"Yup," answered Flounder.

Inside the ship, Ariel found an old steamer trunk. "Look at this!" she cried, holding up a purple parasol.

"And this!" Coral exclaimed, picking up a fancy lamp shade. "I wonder what it's for?"

"My friend Scuttle can tell us," Ariel said. "Follow me!"

"Where are we going?" Coral asked Flounder.

"To the surface," he replied matter-of-factly.

Before Coral had time to be scared, the friends had arrived. Scuttle the seagull was perched on a rock. He examined their treasures. "That is a scribbleflow," he said, looking at Ariel's parasol. "Small humans use them to paddle around in the ocean."

Then he turned his attention to Coral's lamp shade. "Oh!" he said with excitement. "A twirleriffer! It's what human ladies wear when they're going somewhere important."

Before long, the friends had to leave.

As they headed home, Coral asked Ariel if she could keep the twirleriffer at the grotto. "It might get lost or broken at home," she explained.

"Of course," Ariel agreed. "The grotto is my secret place, and it can be yours, too."

A few days later, when Ariel swam to the grotto, she heard someone singing. The voice was strong and clear—but sweet, too.

When Ariel looked into the grotto, she saw her new friend.

"Coral!" Ariel cried. "I didn't know you could sing!"

"I can't," Coral said. "Not like you."

"Nonsense! You have a lovely voice!" Ariel declared. "You should be singing in the concert, not playing the cymbals."

The little blond mermaid shrugged. "I just like singing to myself," she explained. "I've never actually performed."

The next day at rehearsal, Sebastian made Ariel and the orchestra practice over and over again, but something always seemed to go wrong.

"The big day is tomorrow!" the crab fretted. "This concert must be fit for a king—King Triton, to be exact! Let's try it again." So they did—and the rehearsal went on and on.

By the end of the afternoon, everyone was tired. "See you tomorrow," Ariel said. Her voice was raspy.

On the day of the concert, Ariel could only whisper. She had lost her voice!

Ariel went to tell Sebastian the news.

"It's my fault," Sebastian moaned. "Yesterday's rehearsal was too long! Now who's going to sing the solo?"

Ariel motioned for Sebastian to follow her. Then she led him to the grotto, where Coral was singing. Sebastian asked the blond mermaid to take Ariel's place.

"Me?" Coral said. "But I can't!"

"You must!" Sebastian insisted. "Otherwise King Triton's birthday celebration will be ruined!"

"I can't sing in front of a crowd of merpeople," Coral pleaded. "And I certainly can't sing in front of King Triton!"

"Sure you can," Flounder said.

Coral thought about how she had visited a sunken ship and gone to the surface, things she had never thought she could do—all because of Ariel. Now her new friend was counting on her.

"All right," Coral said slowly. "I'll do it."

That night, when Coral peeked out from backstage, she nearly fainted. The entire kingdom was there—including her parents and all of her brothers and sisters! King Triton and Ariel sat in the royal box.

When it was time, Coral took a deep breath and swam onstage. As the orchestra started playing, she sang softly. But as her confidence grew, Coral's voice got louder. Before she knew it, the concert was over, and the audience began to clap and cheer.

"Coral," said Sebastian, smiling broadly. "You can give away your cymbals. From now on, you're going to be a court singer!"

After the show, Ariel went backstage to congratulate her friend. She found Coral with her family.

"I didn't know you could sing like that!" one of Coral's sisters exclaimed.

"No one ever would have known if it wasn't for Ariel," replied Coral. "She believed in me, and that helped me believe in myself."

Ariel still couldn't speak, but she smiled at Coral and gave her a big hug. She was glad everything had worked out so well. It had been a wonderful evening.

Beauty and the Beast

Just Say Please

One rainy day in the Beast's library, Belle and a little teacup named Chip were playing a game called Treasure Hunt. Each clue led to another—the last one to a treat.

Belle picked up the first card and read it, "Take a look in the big red book."

"There's a big red book on the table!" Chip said excitedly.

Drops of water splashed around them. The roof on the Beast's old castle was so full of leaks that it seemed to be raining inside!

Belle dodged the drops of water and pulled a card from inside the red book. "It says, 'Let's have a race to a warm, snug place.'"

"It must be near the fireplace!" Chip cried.

Belle removed a card that was tacked behind a picture over the mantel.

"The clue says, 'Under the rug is a great big . . .'"
Belle read.

"A great big what?" asked Chip.

"That's all it says," Belle said. "If you find the last clue,
you'll get the answer."

Chip bounced around the room until he found a card
under the rug.

"It says, HUG!" Belle exclaimed. "That's your treat!"
Then she gave him a big hug.

"Treasure Hunt is lots of fun," Chip said happily. "You know, if the Beast played games once in a while, I bet he wouldn't be so grumpy all the time."

"Why don't you ask him to play sometime?" Belle suggested.

"All right," Chip agreed.

Just then they heard the whistle of a teakettle.

"Mama is making tea," Chip said. "I'll go and see if she's made tea cakes, too!"

Belle settled down to read. Her book had fallen under the cushion. As she pulled it out, she felt something else.

It was a piece of string with two keys on it. I wonder what these are for, she thought. I'll ask the Beast later. She put the keys in her pocket and began to read.

Meanwhile, in the kitchen, Mrs. Potts, the teapot, was trying to make some cakes—but water was dripping everywhere.

"These leaks are awful," she told Lumiere, the candelabrum.

"I've been begging the Beast to repair the roof for weeks," he replied.

Suddenly Chip rushed in. "Mama, Mama!" he called.

"Hello, dear," Mrs. Potts said. "You know, it isn't polite to interrupt. And if you do, you should say '*excuse me.*'"

"Excuse me," Chip said. "May I have a tea cake?"

"May I have a tea cake, what?" asked Mrs. Potts.

"Um . . . may I have a cake, *please*?"

"Of course, dear," his mother said.

"Thank you," Chip replied.

119

Just then, the Beast burst into the room. He grabbed three cakes without saying *please* or *thank you.*

"I need tools to repair the roof," he said grumpily as he gobbled the cakes up. "But I can't find the keys to the toolshed."

"I'll look for them, Master," said Lumiere. He scurried off to search for the keys.

"Would you like to play Treasure Hunt with Belle and me sometime?" Chip asked the Beast shyly. "It's a fun game that Belle invented."

"Not now. I need to find those keys," the Beast said impatiently. He took three more cakes and stomped off.

A little while later, Chip brought a cake to Belle. "Thank you," Belle said. "That was very sweet of you."

"Belle, is it all right that the Beast isn't polite because he owns the castle?" Chip asked.

"Everyone should try to be polite," Belle answered. "But it's easy to forget." She and Chip decided to try to be extrathoughtful so that the Beast would notice and be polite himself.

That night Chip helped his mother serve dinner. "Would you like some more potatoes, Belle?" he asked.

"Yes, please, Chip," Belle replied. "Thank you!"

"Excuse me while I bring in more gravy," said Chip.

"I'm proud of Chip for being so polite," Belle told the Beast.

But the Beast didn't seem to be listening. He was too busy wolfing down his food.

Drip, drop. The ceiling began to leak again. "These confounded leaks must be fixed!" the Beast shouted. "Cogsworth! Lumiere!" he bellowed. "I need you in the dining room—*now!*"

The mantel clock and the candelabrum came running in. "Have you seen the keys to the toolshed?" the Beast demanded. "Two small keys on a piece of string?"

They told him they hadn't.

Belle remembered the two keys in her pocket. She knew the Beast wanted them, but she also thought he could be a little nicer to everyone.

All of a sudden, she had an idea.

She whispered her plan to Chip. He grinned and nodded. Then Belle stood up.

"Excuse me," she said. "But Chip and I want everyone to join us in the ballroom in a few minutes for a special treasure hunt."

"Not now!" the Beast growled.

"It will be worth it," Belle assured the Beast. "I promise."

Once everyone had gathered in the ballroom, Belle explained the game. "On each card there's a clue to help you find the next card. Each clue also ends with a missing rhyming word."

The Beast tapped his foot impatiently.

"I'll read the first one," Belle said, pulling a card from her pocket. "It says, 'To see your face is why you use me. To interrupt, you say . . .'"

"Excuse me!" called Chip.

"Good, Chip!" exclaimed Mrs. Potts. "You use a mirror to see your face. I think the next clue is behind the frame!"

Mrs. Potts took down the card and read, "'A knight in armor clinks and clanks. When someone's nice, we should say . . .'"

"Thanks!" Cogsworth and Lumiere shouted at the same time.

"This is a waste of time!" the Beast protested. He started to stomp out of the room, but Belle put her hand on his arm.

"Wait one minute," she said. "Please."

The Beast hesitated, then he nodded.

Cogsworth took a card from the suit of armor by the door. Lumiere read, "'Missing keys are found with ease, if you remember to just say . . .'"

Everyone's eyes were on the Beast. Now he understood that the treasure hunt was Belle's way of helping him to be polite. He shuffled his feet.

Finally, he smiled. "*Please?*" he asked Belle.

Belle smiled back and held out the keys. The Beast took them and turned to leave the room. But then he turned back.

"I almost forgot," he said. "*Thank you,* Belle."

"*You're welcome,*" she replied happily and winked at Chip.

The next day, the Beast repaired the leaky roof. Cogsworth
and Lumiere helped him. All day, the Beast remembered to be
polite. He said *please* and *thank you* constantly.

By late afternoon, all the leaks were repaired.

"What a relief!" Mrs. Potts exclaimed when the Beast had finished.

"Thank you for mending the roof," Cogsworth said to the Beast.

"*Oui, merci*," Lumiere added.

"You're welcome," the Beast replied with a grin.

Aim to Please

"We're back!" cried Cinderella. Through the carriage window, she looked at the beautiful castle excitedly.

"Welcome home," the Prince said with a smile.

Cinderella and the Prince had been married a couple of weeks earlier, and they were just getting back from their honeymoon.

"I still can't believe I'm going to live in a castle," Cinderella said. "Are you sure this isn't just a dream?"

The Prince chuckled. "You're a princess now!" he told her.

Inside the castle, the King heard that his son and Cinderella had returned from their trip. He summoned Prudence, who ran the royal household, and asked her to teach Cinderella about her new responsibilites.

"It's going to be your duty to prepare the girl," the King said. "The royal banquet will be Cinderella's responsibility now."

Prudence was horrified. That had always been her job!

Cinderella and the Prince stepped out of the carriage and headed toward the castle. But the King met them halfway and told the Prince that he had to leave at once. "We have important matters to attend to."

"Now?" the Prince said. "Father, I can't just abandon my princess. Not with the royal banquet only two days away. She hasn't had time to prepare!"

"Your Majesty," offered Prudence, "I can take care of the preparations, as always."

"Just show Cinderella what to do," the King ordered. "It's her duty to plan the banquet." He hurried into the carriage.

"I'm sorry to rush off," said the Prince.

"Don't worry," Cinderella replied confidently, "I'll be fine."

But the next morning, the princess wasn't so sure.

Prudence found Cinderella making breakfast in her old clothes. "A princess never prepares her own meals," Prudence said. "That is not how things are done." She made Cinderella leave the kitchen and change into a gown.

Later, Cinderella's mouse friends Jaq and Gus listened with interest as Prudence described the menu to the princess: roast beef, tarragon mashed potatoes, and French onion soup. The mice wondered what was for dessert.

"Stewed prunes," Prudence announced. She pointed to prunes that had been shaped into a cake.

"Prunes?" Cinderella said in disbelief.

"The King expects them," Prudence replied. "It is a tradition that has never been broken."

Later that morning, Cinderella spotted the baker, the flower seller, and some of the other villagers at the castle gates. "My friends!" she cried happily.

"Open the gates!" Cinderella called to the guard.

"No, no!" Prudence scolded. "You must remember the rules. Commoners are never allowed in the palace. It simply isn't done!"

Cinderella looked at her friends sadly and followed Prudence back to the castle.

Prudence gave Cinderella more and more rules to follow. Every time the princess had an idea for the banquet, Prudence said the same thing: "It simply isn't done."

That afternoon, the servants tried to help Cinderella by quizzing her about the rules. "Gold or silver?" they asked. "Fish or fowl? Stand or sit? Left or right?"

"I-I don't know!" Cinderella cried.

Prudence made the princess practice the King's favorite dance with a stack of books on her head. After a couple of hours, she got tired and fell. The books clattered to the floor.

Prudence didn't care. "Your Highness," she said sternly, "the dance is best performed on one's feet."

Cinderella glared at her and went upstairs.

Once she was in her room, Cinderella began to cry. Jaq and Gus tried to comfort her. The princess told them that she didn't agree with Prudence's rules, especially the one about keeping commoners out of the palace. "Why, I was a dish maid when the Prince married me!" she cried.

Suddenly, Cinderella realized that she didn't need to obey anyone's silly rules about how to be a princess. "I'm going to plan this banquet my way!" Cinderella told the mice. "I know I can do this," she said. "I just have to stop trying to be someone else."

The next morning, Cinderella marched outside wearing comfortable clothes and her hair in a ponytail. "Open the gates!" she cried out.

She walked through the village, passing out invitations to the butcher, the baker, and the flower seller—dear friends she had known all her life. Prudence was horrified.

When she returned to the castle, Cinderella headed straight for the kitchen. "This party needs help, starting with dessert!" she said.

"No prunes!" Gus cried. *"Yecchh!"* Then Jaq knocked over a container of chocolate.

"Chocolate pudding!" declared Cinderella. It was absolutely perfect for dessert!

Cinderella's next stop was the ballroom. She told the orchestra to play a lively waltz at the banquet.

Suddenly, Prudence stormed into the ballroom. "It simply isn't done!" she said with a gasp.

Cinderella tried to reassure her. "I know this is a big change," she said. "But I have to try things my way."

"Well, then," said Prudence, "I certainly hope you know what you're doing."

Later that day, Cinderella put on her favorite dress and necklace. It was almost time for the banquet. "It's too late to turn back now," she said. Cinderella went downstairs to the ballroom. The orchestra was playing a merry tune. The royal guests and commoners had arrived and were dancing together like the best of friends.

All at once, the trumpets sounded. The King and the Prince had returned! Cinderella had butterflies in her stomach. What would the King say? She held her breath as he walked in. He stopped and stared. Commoners in the palace? The orchestra playing a waltz?

At that moment, a servant ran by with a big silver bowl. *Smack!* She bumped right into the King. The bowl landed on his head! *Splat!*

"What the blazes is going on here?" the King bellowed.

"This is all Cinderella's doing!" cried Prudence, standing nearby. "I tried to teach her, but she refused to listen!"

The King pointed to his head. "And what is this?"

"Your dessert, sire," whispered Cinderella.

"No prunes?" he cried angrily.

All the servants and guests were staring at the King nervously. Even the orchestra had stopped playing. The King tasted the pudding. "Mmmm! Chocolate. My favorite!" Suddenly, he began to laugh! "What happened to the music?" he called out.

Just then, the Prince arrived. He swept Cinderella into his arms and whirled her around the dance floor.

After a moment, the royal couple noticed that the King was shaking Prudence's hand and complimenting her. "I always said we needed some new traditions around here. Go on now, Prudence, you're missing all the fun." Then the King pushed Prudence into the Grand Duke's arms, and the two began to dance across the floor.

The Prince looked around and noticed all the changes. "Did I miss something?" he asked.

Cinderella smiled and told him that she'd tried to be true to who she was as she planned the banquet.

When Prudence and the Grand Duke passed by again, the King was still talking about how wonderfully everything had turned out.

"It is the princess who deserves your praise, sire," Prudence told him. "And I am honored to be at Her Highness's service."

Cinderella looked at Prudence and smiled. "I think we're going to be great friends."

Gus, Jaq, and the other mice watched from the balcony. They were glad everything had gone so well for Cinderella, and they'd been having a wonderful time, too.

"I told my son he had chosen well," the King said delightedly, as he escorted Cinderella and the Prince to their thrones. "You're a natural!"

The King placed a glittering crown onto Cinderella's head.

"Hooray!" everyone cheered, including the mice.

"I'm glad you did things your own way," the Prince told Cinderella.

She blushed. "Someday I'll get this princess thing right."

The Prince leaned over and gave Cinderella a kiss.

"I think that day is today," he answered with a smile.

WALT DISNEY'S
Sleeping Beauty

The Fairies Plan a Wedding

The fairies Flora, Fauna, and Merryweather had loved Princess Aurora from the time she was a baby. Now the princess was engaged to marry her true love, Prince Phillip, and the fairies couldn't have been happier.

"It's going to be a beautiful wedding," Fauna said as she watched the young couple stroll through the castle gardens.

"Of course it is! We're going to make sure of that," Flora said.

"What do you mean?" asked Fauna.

"Well," Flora began, "we can't trust just anyone with the preparations for the wedding. We must see to them ourselves!"

"You're right," Merryweather agreed. "We must go to the king and queen and ask them to put us in charge!"

King Stefan and the queen agreed right away.

"It would be an honor to have you take care of the wedding," the queen said graciously.

That afternoon, the fairies made a list of everything that needed to be done.

"Invitations have to be made, addressed, and delivered," Flora began.

"We'll need to create a beautiful bouquet for the bride," Fauna continued.

"And a spectacular cake," Merryweather added.

"Don't forget the music and Princess Aurora's gown," Flora reminded them.

The list got longer and longer. When it was finally done, the fairies looked outside and saw stars in the sky. It was nighttime! "Oh, my!" said Flora. "We'd better get some sleep—we've got lots of work to do!"

The next day, the fairies rose early, ready to get to work.

"Let's begin with the flowers," Flora suggested.

The other fairies agreed. Soon they were in the royal garden. Every flower imaginable grew there. Flora wanted the princess to carry roses. Merryweather thought that was a bad idea—the stems had such prickly thorns. But there were too many choices.

"There's plenty of time to decide," Merryweather said. "Why don't we go see about the invitations instead?"

Together, the fairies went to a room in the castle that was filled with fancy paper.

"I like this," said Fauna, holding up a sheet of creamy yellow.

"Oh, no, this is much better!" Flora replied, waving some pink paper that had a scalloped edge.

"Wedding invitations should always be white," disagreed Merryweather. "I'm sure the princess thinks so, too!"

"Dears," Fauna interrupted, "let's not bicker. There's plenty of time to settle on the invitations. Why don't we go see about the wedding cake instead?"

In the kitchen, Flora, Fauna, and Merryweather argued about what kind of cake to make.

"Ladies," the baker said gently, "why don't you come back when you decide?"

Next, the fairies went to meet Princess Aurora at the royal dressmaker's. When they arrived, the princess greeted them warmly. "Isn't this lovely?" she asked, holding up some ivory-colored satin.

"It *is* pretty, dear," Flora agreed, "but what about this silk?" She circled Merryweather, covering her in fabric.

"Or how about velvet?" Fauna asked, winding more cloth around Merryweather.

Flora, Fauna, and the princess kept wrapping different fabrics around Merryweather. Soon the weight of the fabric was too much, and Merryweather fell over.

"If no one minds," she said, "could we choose the fabric another day?"

The search for just the right music to play at the wedding didn't go any better. The royal musicians played song after song for the fairies, but Flora, Fauna, and Merryweather simply couldn't agree.

The day before the wedding, the three fairies met to go over what still needed to be done. "Let's see," Fauna said, "the list says invitations, flowers, food, wedding cake, music, and wedding gown."

"But . . . but . . . that's almost everything!" Merryweather cried.

"I'll never forgive myself!" Flora wailed. "We've ruined the princess's wedding!"

"Wait!" Fauna said, her face suddenly brightening. "There's still time to arrange a magnificent wedding—we'll just use magic."

"What a perfect plan!" agreed Flora.

"We're going to have to give our wands double the power to get everything done!" Fauna said. "Be back here in an hour to make the wedding gown."

And with that, the fairies took out their wands and hurried off.

Merryweather went straight to the room with the fancy paper and waved her wand. "Invitations make yourselves, then fly down from all your shelves!" she commanded. Within seconds, hundreds of pieces of paper folded themselves and pens began to write out the details.

Then the invitations flew out the window, landing on doorsteps throughout the kingdom.

Meanwhile, Fauna went to the kitchen and asked the royal baker to bring out the cake he had made for that night's dessert.

Fauna concentrated on the simple cake before her. When she waved her wand over it, she said, "Make this cake grand, so that it might feed all the land!"

Immediately, the cake began to grow. Soon it had gotten as big as the table it was on!

"Perfect!" Fauna exclaimed as she scurried off to her next task.

Outside, Flora flew over the garden. She smiled at her wand and said, "Send your magic down below and make Aurora's bouquet grow!" Then she chuckled. "By the time I return, the princess will have the most beautiful bouquet of flowers! But first, I'd better meet Merryweather and Fauna. I don't want them to make the wedding dress without me!"

Flora, Fauna, and Merryweather took a simple dress from Princess Aurora's closet. The fairies held their wands over the dress. Flora closed her eyes and began, "Make a gown for a lovely bride—"

And Fauna finished, "—with a train that's long and wide."

Then Merryweather added one last thing, "And since you are three wands, not one, we expect a job well done!"

A swirl of fairy dust surrounded the dress for a moment, then disappeared. What stood before them was an exquisite gown. But its train was so long it stretched across the floor, out the window—and clear to the other side of the kingdom!

Just then, Princess Aurora appeared carrying a bouquet of weeds. "I found these in the garden," she said. "Then she caught sight of the wedding gown. "And what happened to that dress?"

Suddenly, there was a loud crash. Moments later, the royal baker rushed in. "The cake is still growing—and it just broke through the roof!"

"We're sorry, Princess!" Flora cried. "We couldn't agree on anything, so we used magic to get everything done in time. But

we made our wands work so quickly that the magic came out all wrong!"

The princess smiled. "Let's postpone the wedding," she offered.

"The invitations have already been sent," said Fauna.

Princess Aurora just smiled and held up an invitation that had landed in the garden. All the letters on it were backward!

"Well, we certainly made a mess of things," Merryweather admitted.

"But I think I know what to do!" Flora said. Then she told the other two fairies her plan.

Soon the fairies were using their magic to put everyone to sleep. Next they turned back the calendars so that it was weeks before the wedding. When they woke everyone up, no one in the kingdom had any idea what had happened.

The fairies sat together, composing a list of preparations for the wedding. First, they chose roses and violets for the princess's bouquet. Then, they decided on a recipe for the wedding cake and also settled on the perfect song to play as Aurora walked down the aisle.

The next week, they addressed the invitations. When they were through, they began choosing the fabric and pattern for Aurora's gown.

A week later, Princess Aurora stopped by with the king and queen.

"Try on your gown," Merryweather suggested.

Aurora put on the pink-and-white gown and twirled around. "I love it!" she cried.

"So the preparations are going well, then?" the queen asked.

The fairies looked at one another, trying hard not to giggle. "Um . . . right on schedule, Your Majesty!" exclaimed Fauna.

Disney's Aladdin

Jasmine's Snowy Day

It was very hot in Agrabah. In fact, it was the tenth hot day in a row, and Jasmine was sick of it.

"Wouldn't it be nice to go somewhere different and new—somewhere cool?" the princess asked her pet tiger, Rajah.

Just then, Aladdin and his monkey, Abu, flew toward Jasmine's balcony on Aladdin's Magic Carpet. They overheard the princess talking.

"Oh, Rajah, I wish I could travel to another world," said Jasmine. "A world with . . . snow!"

Aladdin decided to go to the Genie for help. "The princess is unhappy, Genie," he said. "Is there any way you could make it snow here? I think that would make her feel a lot better."

"I'm on the job, Al!" said the Genie. "With a poof, a puff, and a ta-da, I'll bring snow to Agrabah!"

When Jasmine woke up the next morning, she could not believe her eyes—Agrabah was a winter wonderland! Glistening snow covered the city. It was actually cool outside! Jasmine went into the palace and found a jacket.

Suddenly, Aladdin, Abu, and the Genie appeared.

"Do you like my surprise?" Aladdin said. "I asked the Genie to cover Agrabah in snow for a day."

"Oh, it's wonderful!" Jasmine cried. "The city is like a whole new world. It's such a nice break from the heat."

"Told you she'd like it, Al!" the Genie said proudly.

"You were right, Genie," Aladdin said. He turned to Jasmine. "Want to go for a ride?

Jasmine jumped onto the Magic Carpet, ready for her snowy adventure.

"Welcome aboard the SS *Snowbound*," said the Genie. "We hope you enjoy your trip."

First, they went to the snow-covered pyramids. Aladdin and Jasmine decided to go sledding. "*Woo-hoo!*" Aladdin yelled as they sped down the side of the tallest pyramid.

"Hey, kids, look out!" shouted the Genie. "A lean, mean skiing machine is about to pass you!" Then he whizzed by on skis.

Next, Jasmine and Aladdin built a castle out of snow. A few minutes later, the Genie and the princess began to whisper to one another.

All of a sudden, they started throwing snowballs at Aladdin.

"Heads up, Abu!" Aladdin warned as he began throwing snowballs back.

"Oh!" Jasmine exclaimed as some snow got her in the neck. But she laughed in delight as her next snowball hit Aladdin right on the elbow.

At first, Abu hopped onto Aladdin's head, but then he saw how much fun everyone was having and began to throw some tiny snowballs of his own. He even hit the Genie in the nose!

A little later, Aladdin and Abu built a giant snowman.

"If I didn't know any better, I'd say that was a genie," the Genie said. "A handsome guy, but he'd look better in blue."

Nearby, Jasmine flopped onto the ground and began to make a snow angel.

When she got up, Jasmine noticed she was getting cold. "*Brrr*," she said. "I almost wish for the heat of the desert again."

"Well, the sun is starting to set," Aladdin said. "Maybe we should go back."

They hopped on the Magic Carpet and flew back to the palace. "Hey, Princess," the Genie said when they landed, "this ought to warm you up." In the blink of an eye, he'd made a fire.

173

"What a splendid day!" Jasmine exclaimed as she and Aladdin sat by the fire. "It was just what I needed. Thank you so much."

"Anything to make you happy," Aladdin replied.

Everyone enjoyed a few more minutes by the fire. Their wonderful snowy day had come to an end.

Dreams Under the Sea

Ariel's secret grotto was her favorite place in the sea. It was where she kept all the objects that she'd found from the world above. She was fascinated with humans, even though her father forbade her to have anything to do with them.

During her last trip to the surface, Ariel had rescued a handsome prince named Eric when a terrible storm sank his ship. She had fallen in love with him, but since he was human, she left before he could see her.

A while later, Ariel's fish friend Flounder found a statue of Eric and surprised the mermaid with it. She swam over to the statue and began to talk to it.

"Ariel!" cried Sebastian, a crab who was her father's adviser. "Get ahold of yourself. That's not a human, it's a hunk of rock!"

Ariel ignored him. "The statue said that if you two would please excuse us, he has something he'd like to say to me."

Ariel placed her head on the statue's shoulder and pretended to answer him. "Why, yes, I'd love to marry you, Eric."

"Marry?" Sebastian roared as he swam back into the grotto. "You will do no such thing. In the name of his royal highness, King Triton, I forbid this kind of talk."

"Oh, Sebastian," Ariel said impatiently, "it's a statue, remember? I'm just pretending. Don't worry, and please don't tell my father, okay?"

Sebastian reluctantly shook his head. "I just know I'm going to regret this," he moaned.

"We can have the wedding right here in the grotto," Ariel said. "There's so much to do! You'll both help me, won't you?"

"Help you with what?" Sebastian asked as Ariel handed him some seaweed to decorate with. "It's make-believe. You said so yourself."

"Oh, dream weddings are every bit as much work as real ones," Ariel insisted. "Everything has to be just right!"

"I think Prince Eric is dressed perfectly for a wedding," Ariel continued.

"This will never work! The real Prince Eric is human," Sebastian said. "He lives on land! And every self-respecting sea dweller knows that mermaids live underwater!"

"That may be true," said Ariel. "But who knows what the future will bring?"

"May I be the chef?" Flounder asked. "Please, please?"

Ariel laughed. "Of course, Flounder," she said. "I want you to prepare all the most wonderful foods you can imagine."

"How about some seaweed soufflé? And some plankton salad?" Flounder asked.

"Oh, yes!" Ariel cried as she imagined the feast. "And don't forget the wedding cake!"

"Just leave it to me," Flounder said proudly.

"This will be a wedding dinner like no one has ever seen!"

"You can say that again," Sebastian muttered.

"Oh, I can hardly wait!" Ariel exclaimed. "I can picture the entire ceremony. My sisters will make such beautiful bridesmaids. And my father will look so proud and distinguished as we—"

"Your father?!" Sebastian looked as if he was ready to faint.

"Oh, don't be such a party pooper, Sebastian," Ariel said lightly. "I'm not actually going to invite my family since this is a pretend wedding."

"At least for now,"
she added quietly.

"That's it!" Sebastian
cried. "I can't take any
more of this nonsense!"

"Flounder!" Ariel called.
"Sebastian's leaving. Can
you think of someone else
who could be the master
conductor of the grand
orchestra?"

"Grand orchestra?"
Sebastian asked. "Master
conductor?"

"Of course you're my first choice,
Sebastian," Ariel said. "But—

183

"*But* nothing!" Sebastian cried. "A crab must do what a crab must do. The pretend wedding *must* go on!"

Grabbing a candlestick from Ariel, Sebastian began to conduct his pretend orchestra.

"May I have this dance?" Flounder asked the little mermaid, bowing politely.

"With pleasure, kind sir!" Ariel laughed. She and Flounder danced, twirling around until they were both dizzy.

That evening, Ariel was trying on a veil she had made when Flounder arrived with a pearl necklace.

"Oh, Flounder, it's beautiful!" Ariel gasped with delight.

"It belongs to a friend," Flounder said. "She said you could borrow it."

Ariel looked around. With the dinglehopper she used to comb her hair, she had something old. The veil she'd just made was something new. The pearls were her something borrowed. And a shell bracelet she'd found was her something blue.

"That's everything a bride needs!" Ariel exclaimed.

The next morning, Sebastian nervously followed Ariel as she made her way to the grotto.

"I hope no one sees us," he said.

"Not getting cold feet—uh, claws—are you?" Ariel teased.

"Most assuredly not," Sebastian retorted. "The orchestra is ready when you are."

"Are you ready?" Flounder asked when Ariel and Sebastian arrived at the grotto. The mermaid nodded, and the fish escorted her down the aisle as the orchestra played the "Wedding March."

Then a funny thing happened—Sebastian began to sniffle.

Ariel turned around in surprise.

"Weddings always make me cry," the crab said with a shrug.

Then Sebastian cleared his throat and moved to the front of the grotto. "Do you, Princess Ariel, take this . . . er . . . this statue to be your—now listen closely to this part, young lady—*make-believe* husband?"

"I do!" Ariel cried happily.

"And do you, Mr. Pretend Prince, take this princess to be your make-believe wife?" Sebastian finished.

Ariel leaned toward the statue. "He says he does," she told the crab with a giggle.

"Well, then, I suppose I have to pronounce you imaginary husband and wife," Sebastian said.

"Hooray!" Flounder cheered.

189

With her eyes glowing like stars, Ariel hugged her friends. "Oh, thank you! This has been a wonderful pretend wedding!" she cried. "And now I'm inviting you both to my real wedding to Prince Eric. I'm not sure when it will happen—or where or how—but I know it will. It won't matter that there's an ocean of difference between us. Nothing can stand in the way of true love."

Ariel sighed with happiness, imagining that she was really marrying Eric. At the end of the ceremony, they would kiss. . . .

"*Ewwwwwwww!*" she cried suddenly. She realized that she was actually kissing a very startled Flounder!

"Aha!" Sebastian shouted. "See what comes of thinking a mermaid could marry a human prince? As if that could ever really happen . . ."

But Ariel didn't care what Sebastian said. She knew in her heart that someday she and Eric would live happily ever after.

WALT DISNEY'S
Snow White
and the Seven Dwarfs

The Mixed-up Morning

One bright, sunny morning, Snow White was in the Seven Dwarfs' kitchen making breakfast.

She stirred a big pot over the fire. "Mmm," she said, as she sniffed it. "The porridge is done. Once I toast the bread, everything will be ready."

"*Tweet! Tweet!*" the birds sang as Snow White sliced some bread.

"Oh, you want breakfast, too," Snow White said with a laugh.

She scooped up a handful of bread crumbs, and one by one, the birds flew over and ate them out of her hand.

When the birds had finished, Snow White ran to the stairs. "Sleepy, Grumpy, Doc, Bashful, Dopey, Sneezy, Happy!" she called. "Breakfast is ready!"

The Dwarfs yawned and stretched. "Mmm," Happy said. "That toast smells wonderful!"

"Well, I'm hungrier than anyone," Grumpy said with a grunt, "so I'm going to wash first."

"No," said Doc. "I want to fo gurst—I mean, *go first!*"

Grumpy and Doc both tugged at the wash bucket. But it flew out of their hands and across the room, landing on Dopey's head. The water poured all over him—he was soaked!

"Oops! Sorry, Dopey!" Doc apologized.

"I told you I should go first!" Grumpy shouted. "What a mess!"

A little while later, Happy wandered over to the dresser. "I need the comb," he announced.

"No, I do," Sneezy insisted.

The two Dwarfs both grabbed the comb and began to use it at the same time.

Happy and Sneezy looked in the mirror. Their beards had gotten knotted together!

"Oh, no!" Sneezy exclaimed.

"Now what will we do?" cried Happy.

As they tried to untangle themselves, Sneezy let loose a gigantic sneeze. *Aa-choo!*

It was such a big sneeze that Happy flew across the room. At last, they were separated.

The rest of the Dwarfs rushed to the mirror, trying to get ready. "You're in my way!" Grumpy snapped at Sleepy.

"That's *my* hat!" Sleepy told Bashful with a yawn.

"Uh, that's *my* jacket," Bashful said to Happy.

"What a mix-up!" Happy remarked.

A few moments later, Snow White called, "Hurry—your breakfast is getting cold!"

The Dwarfs raced to the stairs, each trying to be the first to get to the table. They bumped into each other and bounced all the way down the stairs.

"Whose foot is on my head?" Sleepy asked.

"You're mitting on see!" Doc mumbled. "I mean, *you're sitting on me!*"

"What a muddle!" groaned Sneezy.

The Dwarfs scrambled into their seats. Sneezy and Happy reached for the milk at the same time. Grumpy and Doc both tried to spoon porridge into their bowls. And Dopey and Sleepy tugged at the same piece of toast.

"Miss is a thess—I mean, *this is a mess*!" cried Doc. All the other Dwarfs quieted down.

"It certainly is," Snow White agreed. "See what happens when you don't take turns? Why don't you clean this mess up, and I'll get you some more breakfast."

After the Dwarfs straightened up, Snow White handed each of them a slice of bread with jam. "Don't worry," she said. "There's enough for everyone."

They ate quietly and thanked Snow White.

When the Dwarfs had eaten, they gathered their things for work. They were headed to the diamond mines.

Doc took his lantern, Grumpy hoisted his pickax, and Sleepy got his shovel. Happy picked up his hammer, while Dopey found a bucket. Sneezy got his rope, and Bashful grabbed some work gloves.

All the Dwarfs got to the front door at the same time.

"Me first!" grumbled Grumpy, shoving the others.

"No, me first," said Happy.

Snow White watched as the Dwarfs all tried to scramble through the door. Instead, they just got stuck.

Oh, dear, Snow White said to herself. I think I better say something.

"Everyone can't fit through at once," she told the Dwarfs.

Dopey wriggled out of the doorway and sat down in the kitchen. The other Dwarfs followed.

"Look what happened this morning when you all tried to do everything at the same time," Snow White said. "Why don't you try it again—one at a time?"

"That's a great idea!" shouted Grumpy. "One at a time. But I'll go first!"

"Oh, no, you don't!" said Sneezy. "*I'll* go first!"

"No, *me*!" cried Happy.

"Oh, dear!" Snow White said, shaking her head. "Everyone can't always be first. You'll have to take turns."

"Hmm," Grumpy mumbled, scratching his beard. "How do we do that?"

"There are seven days in a week, right?" Snow White said.

"Well, yes," said Doc

"And there are seven of you, right?" she asked

Dopey started to count, became confused, and started again.

"Yes, there are seven of us," Happy said.

"So every week, each of you will have his own special day to be first!" Snow White explained. "Here, Bashful," she said, handing him a basket filled with lunch. "Today is your day to be first."

Bashful blushed. "Thanks," he said shyly.

One by one, the Dwarfs walked outside. Snow White waved good-bye as they happily marched off to work. The mixed-up morning had ended nicely after all.

Beauty and the Beast

Getting to Know You

Maybe the Beast does have a heart, thought Belle. That very day, he had rescued her from a pack of wolves in the forest. Even though the Beast was angry with Belle for having left the castle against his orders, he had risked his life to save hers.

"Perhaps I could try a little harder to be his friend," she told herself.

Mrs. Potts the teapot, Lumiere the candelabrum, and Cogsworth the mantel clock were hopeful. If the Beast and Belle fell in love, the spell that had turned the servants into household objects would be broken—and they and the Beast would be human again!

Belle put a blanket over the Beast, but he didn't say anything.

That night, Mrs. Potts went to see the Beast. "Master, it's such a chilly night," she began. "Wouldn't you like a nice, hot drink in front of the fireplace? I'm sure Belle would love some company."

Reluctantly, the Beast stomped into the sitting room and settled into a chair. Mrs. Potts poured him some hot chocolate.

Belle looked up from where she sat reading. "Good evening," she said. The Beast did his best to smile politely.

Belle went back to her book. Soon she was startled by a loud slurp. She looked over at the Beast. He had a chocolate mustache. Oh, dear, thought Belle.

The Beast realized he hadn't been very polite. Discouraged, he set his cup down and slumped in his chair.

Mrs. Potts saw what had happened and was determined to get Belle and the Beast to have a nice evening. "Why don't you read to us, Belle?" she suggested.

"All right," Belle agreed. She turned to a new story.

"'Once upon a time there was a woodcutter—'" she began.

"That sounds so boring!" the Beast said, interrupting her. Belle scowled.

"Is there another story, Belle?" Mrs. Potts asked gently.

Belle flipped through the book until she found a tale about fire-breathing dragons and brave knights. Surely, this will be exciting enough, she thought, and she began to read. The Beast sat on the edge of his seat the whole time, listening to every word.

Belle noticed how much the Beast enjoyed the story and that when he started to drink his cocoa again, he took care not to slurp.

The next day, Lumiere and Cogsworth decided to play matchmaker, too.

"What a beautiful day to go for a walk!" Cogsworth said after breakfast. "Look, the sun is shining!"

"What's the point of taking a walk?" challenged the Beast. "Walking is only useful when you have somewhere to go!"

But before Belle and the Beast knew it, they were being bundled up and hurried out the door.

"There's nothing more romantic than a walk in the snow!" Lumiere said dreamily as Belle and the Beast made their way toward the woods.

Belle and the Beast walked along in uncomfortable silence. Then they came to a very large mud puddle.

While Belle tried to figure out how to cross it without getting dirty, the Beast stomped ahead.

A gentleman would carry me over the puddle, Belle thought. It was obvious the Beast wasn't going to, though.

Oh, well, here goes! she thought as she waded through the muck.

Her skirt, coat, and boots got covered in mud.

The Beast turned around to see what was taking Belle so long. He noticed how dirty her pretty outfit had gotten. Oops! he thought to himself. I guess I should have helped her.

The wind picked up, and all at once it started to snow. "It looks as if a bad storm is coming," the Beast warned. "We'd better get back while we can still see where we're going."

Belle nodded. She wrapped her cloak tightly and trudged through the falling snow. She tried to keep up with the Beast, but began to fall behind.

Quite unexpectedly, the Beast took Belle's hand. "Follow me!" he commanded, leading her through the blizzard.

Lumiere and Cogsworth were watching out the window as the two approached. They noticed Belle's hand in the Beast's paw.

"How romantic!" exclaimed Lumiere.

Belle was relieved when they made it to the castle and surprised at the way the Beast had taken care of her.

A few minutes later, Belle went upstairs to change. "It looks as if you and the master are getting to know each other better," Mrs. Potts said.

Belle hesitated. "I suppose," she answered. "There is so much about him that's gruff and rude . . . and yet, he's full of surprises."

In the meantime, in another part of the castle, Cogsworth and Lumiere were helping the Beast dry off.

"Did you have a nice walk, master?" Cogsworth asked.

The Beast hesitated. "Yes," he began. "Belle can be rather boring and proper. But then she walked through the mud without complaining. And she didn't act scared when we got caught in the storm. She's kind of surprising."

That afternoon, Mrs. Potts prepared a lovely lunch and served it in the castle's greenhouse.

"Remember, master," Lumiere whispered as the Beast went to the table, "young ladies appreciate politeness."

"Try to be understanding," Mrs. Potts begged Belle. "The master's manners aren't what they should be—but he's trying!"

When they got to the table, Belle smiled primly, and the Beast managed a grin. Both were getting tired of trying to be on their best behavior.

Their drinks were served, and Belle and the Beast began to eat.

The Beast grabbed a chicken leg and began to devour it.

But after Belle picked up her napkin and placed it in her lap, the Beast grabbed his own napkin and did the same.

"Isn't this lunch delicious?" asked Belle.

"Mmpff," the Beast answered, his mouth stuffed with food.

Just then, the Beast noticed that his napkin had fallen on the floor. He ducked down to retrieve it—and accidentally tipped the table over as he tried to sit back up. A roll flew off his plate and hit Belle in the face!

Uh-oh, thought the Beast. Even he knew that throwing food was not polite. This lunch was a disaster! He was about to apologize when he saw a playful smile on Belle's face. To his surprise, she threw the roll right back at him!

Bonk! It hit him on the ear.

Belle took one look at the Beast's startled expression, and burst out laughing.

When Mrs. Potts, Lumiere, and Cogsworth came to check on the pair, they couldn't believe their eyes. The room was a mess! Food was everywhere—on the floor, in the drapes, on the window. It looked like there had been a food fight. But what was most surprising of all was that Belle and the Beast couldn't stop laughing!

"Ooh la la!" Lumiere exclaimed. "What happened here?"

Mrs. Potts smiled knowingly. "I think they discovered what we forgot: the real way to make friends is to relax and be yourself! It looks like they did just that."

That night, Belle and the Beast got cleaned up and had a wonderful dinner together.

Afterward, Belle patiently taught the Beast how to dance. He listened carefully to everything she told him, and soon the two were gliding across the dance floor . . . in step with each other at last.

Walt Disney's Sleeping Beauty

A Moment to Remember

Princess Aurora sighed. She loved being married to Prince Phillip, but life in the palace was so different than what she was used to. Three kind fairies—Merryweather, Flora, and Fauna—had raised her in a cottage in the woods to protect her from an evil spell. Aurora had done so much there, from cooking and cleaning to going on walks and spending time with her animal friends.

Now that she lived in the palace, it seemed all she did was plan and attend parties. Tonight there would be yet another royal ball, and everyone was fussing over the plans.

The royal chef couldn't decide on an ice sculpture. The royal florist and the table setter couldn't agree on flowers. While they were bickering, Prince Phillip came in. "Hello, dearest," he said.

Aurora beamed and gave him a hug. The table setter and the florist were annoyed at the interruption.

"Princess Aurora," the royal florist said, "could you please tell the royal table setter that she must place the flowers in the middle of each table tonight?"

"Princess Aurora," said the royal table setter, "could you please tell the royal florist that our guests will never see one another if I put his big flower arrangements in the middle of each table?"

"Why don't you just put a single flower on each table?" Aurora suggested.

The two servants looked at her, horrified. "A single flower?" they said.

Phillip cleared his throat. "Ahem," he said.

226

"That will be all, thank you," Aurora told the servants. She turned to Phillip. "It's so good to see—"

"Pardon me, Princess Aurora." The royal steward bowed. "But I must have your approval on the seating arrangements."

"Thank you," said the princess. "I will look at them—"

"As soon as we return," Prince Phillip finished.

Both Aurora and the steward looked at Phillip in surprise.

"Where are we going?" Aurora asked.

Phillip smiled. "Out for a ride—by ourselves."

The princess smiled. It was just what she had been hoping for. Aurora hurried to change her outfit.

As Phillip and Aurora set off, the prince remembered somthing. "I'm sorry, dearest," he said, "I had forgotten that the Royal Equestrian Guards must come with us."

Aurora looked sadly at the ten riders behind them. Then she leaned down and whispered to Phillip's horse, Samson. The horse whinnied and charged away from the palace. Aurora's horse, Mirette, galloped after them. Before long, the Royal Guards were far behind.

"*Whooaa! Whoa, Samson!*" the prince shouted as his horse raced ahead.

"It's all right, Phillip!" Aurora called.

They galloped into the forest and Samson found a path through the trees. He followed it for a while, then stopped very suddenly.

Phillip sailed over Samson's head and landed in a stream.

"No carrots for you, boy!" Prince Phillip scolded his horse.

He looked up and saw Aurora trying to hide a smile. He grinned.

"Do you remember this place?" Aurora asked a little later.

Phillip waded out of the stream and looked around the

clearing. He pulled off his boots and dumped the water out of

them. Then he set them in the sun to dry.

Aurora took off her shoes, too. She spun around gracefully,

humming a tune.

"Yes," Prince Phillip said

softly. "I remember this place.

This is where we first met.

I heard you singing

sweetly, and then we

danced together for

the first time."

"I will never forget that day," said Aurora, "no matter how busy we get with our royal duties."

Prince Phillip smiled. "Nor will I. When I am with you, all others disappear."

Phillip and Aurora smiled, wishing they could bring the peacefulness of the glade back to the palace.

Their peaceful moment ended as the Royal Equestrians thundered into the glade.

Phillip put on his boots and cape. Then he picked up a fallen flower and handed it to Aurora.

Aurora took the gift and smiled. "We should go back and get ready for the ball," she said.

"You go ahead, dear," Phillip said. "I'll be back soon."

Aurora nodded and smiled. On the way back to the palace, she thought of a surprise for her husband.

Meanwhile, Phillip had an idea of his own. "Not a word of this to the princess," he said to her animal friends as he began to gather some flowers.

At the castle, Princess Aurora worked on Phillip's surprise for the rest of the afternoon. Servants moved tables, laid tablecloths, and gathered flowers. Flora, Fauna, and Merryweather flitted about, helping wherever they could.

More than once, Aurora heard a servant murmur, "Our guests will certainly be . . . surprised."

Aurora just smiled. "It is Prince Phillip I want to surprise," she said. "Not a word of this to him."

That night, Aurora had just finished getting dressed when Prince Phillip came into the room. He held out a simple crown he had made from flowers. "Would you like to wear this, too?" he asked.

"Oh, Phillip!" Aurora put on the flower crown and hugged her husband. "It's perfect for this evening. What a lovely gift!"

Aurora took Phillip's hand. "Now I have a surprise for you!" She led the prince down the stairs to the courtyard.

The courtyard was decorated with flowers and trees. Water danced in the fountain. Aurora's woodland friends were there, too.

"The glade will always be in our hearts," Aurora whispered. "But now it is in our palace, too."

Just then Phillip's father, King Hubert, came over.

"This is much better than the stuffy balls I usually attend," he said to Princess Aurora. "Thank you for all your hard work, my dear!"

Phillip took Aurora's hand and led her to the middle of the courtyard. "It *is* beautiful, Aurora. Thank you so much."

Aurora smiled at her husband, and they began to dance. Like the first time they had met, this, too, would be a moment to remember.

DISNEY'S Aladdin

A Magical Surprise

It was a lovely day in Agrabah. The sun shone brightly, and a gentle breeze cooled the desert sands. In the palace garden, Princess Jasmine sat by the fountain and poured some tea for her pet Bengal tiger, Rajah.

Even though it was beautiful outside, Jasmine felt a tiny bit sad.

Rajah knew something was wrong. He looked at the princess worriedly.

Jasmine smiled at the tiger. "Sorry to be so glum," she said. "It's just that I had hoped to spend the day with Aladdin. But he's nowhere to be found. I've looked all over the palace."

Rajah nodded sympathetically. He knew how much she liked spending time with her husband.

"I wonder if he went on an adventure with the Genie and the Magic Carpet," Jasmine said.

Just then, the Magic Carpet zoomed into the garden!

The Magic Carpet came to a stop in front of the tea table.
Then it began to dart around and wave its tasseled corners.
It seemed to be trying to tell Jasmine something.

"What is it?" she asked.

The Magic Carpet did a playful flip. Jasmine could tell it
wanted her to jump aboard.

"Oh, well," the princess said at last. "Since Aladdin's not
around, I might as
well go for a ride."

The Magic
Carpet eagerly
swooped down
and picked her up.
With a quick wave
to Rajah, Jasmine
was off.

"Oh, Magic Carpet, it's beautiful up here!" the princess said happily as the carpet soared into the sky, over the palace, and above the desert. But after she'd been flying for a while, Jasmine began to think about Aladdin. She always rode the Magic Carpet with him.

Jasmine decided to look for her husband, so she asked the Magic Carpet to fly over the city. Yet, nearly an hour later, they still hadn't found Aladdin.

"Do you think we should go home?" Jasmine asked.

The Magic Carpet waved its tassels and turned around.

Soon the Magic Carpet landed in the middle of the palace garden. All at once, Jasmine's friends and family leaped out from behind the shrubs. "Surprise!" they yelled.

"Oh, my!" Jasmine cried excitedly. She spotted Rajah and her father immediately. Then she noticed there were decorations everywhere—the Genie even had a party hat on. It looked like everyone was throwing a party for her.

I wonder what the occasion could be? Jasmine thought. It's not my birthday or a holiday. And I wonder where Aladdin is.

Jasmine heard something behind her. She turned and saw Aladdin standing next to a large cake.

"Happy anniversary!" he cried.

Jasmine smiled. "It's not our anniversary," she whispered.

Aladdin grinned and whispered back, "It's the anniversary of the day we first met in the marketplace. I thought it was cause for a celebration."

Jasmine kissed Aladdin on the cheek. Then the guests began to gather around.

"Happy anniversary, my dear," the Sultan said.

"Yeah, happy anniversary, Jasmine," the Genie said. "When Al told me about this shindig, I broke out my best party hat. Now let's liven this place up!" He snapped his fingers and an orchestra appeared. "Hit it, boys!"

Soon everyone was laughing and dancing. Then they ate some cake, and Jasmine opened her presents.

After a few hours of merriment, the guests began to leave.
Jasmine spotted the Magic Carpet.

"Why, you sneaky thing!" she said. "You were in on the
surprise all along, weren't you?" She ruffled the Magic Carpet's
tassels. Then she leaned in to whisper to it.

Suddenly, the Magic Carpet scooped up Aladdin and Jasmine.

"Whoa!" Aladdin cried as they flew above the garden.

"I just wanted to say thanks," Jasmine said.
"This has been the best
anniversary ever. I'm so
lucky to have such
wonderful friends
and family."

Aladdin smiled at her.
It was a day they would
never forget.

Walt Disney's
Snow White
and the Seven Dwarfs

Two Hearts as One

Snow White kissed her husband, the Prince, as she left the castle. She was going to visit her friends, the Seven Dwarfs. "I'll be back soon," she said.

"I'll miss you," the Prince replied.

Snow White sang happily as she rode into the woods. She

and the Prince were about to celebrate their first wedding anniversary!

That was part of why she was going to see the Dwarfs— so she could work on a gift without her husband finding out about it.

It had been a magical year, and Snow White wanted to surprise him.

"Hello! Hello!" Snow White called to the Seven Dwarfs as she neared their cottage. They had been watching for the princess and ran toward her excitedly. Even Grumpy was delighted!

"I have a special favor to ask you," Snow White said after they had all greeted each other. "The Prince and I will be celebrating our first anniversary soon. I would like to make him a special dinner, but no one at the palace will let me cook!"

"They don't know what they're missin'!" Grumpy said.

Snow White smiled. "I wondered if I could make dinner for him here. I also want to give him a special gift—something he can add to his shield."

"Like a diamond?" said Doc.

Snow White nodded happily. "That would be lovely," she said.

Doc smiled. "Don't you worry, Snow White! I'll cake tare of it—I mean, *take care of it*—myself!"

Grumpy frowned and glared at Doc.

Snow White didn't notice, though. "Oh, thank you," she said. "Now how about some gooseberry pie? I baked it this morning, before the cook woke up."

Snow White took a pie out of the basket she'd brought with her and served it to the Dwarfs.

"Mmm, this pie is delicious!" Happy exclaimed.

After a nice visit, Snow White left. "I'll see you tomorrow," she said. Then she waved to her friends and left for the castle.

Grumpy turned to Doc, "So you don't think the rest of us can find a diamond for Snow White? You didn't even offer to let us help. We'll see about that!" He stomped off by himself.

All night long, Grumpy planned which part of the mine he would search to find the perfect diamond to give to Snow White. He stayed up so late thinking about it that he overslept! By the time he woke up, the other Dwarfs had already left.

"Dag nab it!" shouted Grumpy. He rushed out the door— straight into the Prince!

"Well, hello, Grumpy." The Prince bowed. "I'm glad to find you at home because I have a favor to ask. I love Snow White so much that I want to give her the most precious gift I can find to celebrate our anniversary. I'm having a crown made for her, and I would like to put a beautiful diamond in the center of it."

Grumpy puffed up his chest. "I'll find the most beautiful, dazzlin' diamond in the whole mine!"

"That would be wonderful," the Prince said. "Let's meet here tonight."

Over at the mine, Doc had already found the perfect diamond. Even though the mine was dark, the diamond sparkled brightly. Doc hurried off to find the other Dwarfs and a pickax so he could dig out the precious gem.

Just then, Grumpy rushed into the deepest part of the mine from a different direction. He turned a corner and saw the back part of the same diamond that Doc had found! Grumpy didn't want to smudge the diamond, so he hurried off to find a soft rag.

Even though Doc said *he* was going to find a diamond for
Snow White, the other Dwarfs were looking for one, too. Dopey
smiled as he walked along one of
the mine paths. Then he saw it—
a large, beautiful diamond!
It was the same one Doc
and Grumpy had found,
but Dopey didn't know
that. He used his pickax
to remove the precious
stone, and then he
began to chisel
away at it. He
wanted to make
it perfect for
Snow White.

In the meantime, Doc and Grumpy had both found the other Dwarfs and told them about the diamond. As they got closer, they saw Dopey. "Hey, what's he doing with my diamond?" Grumpy said angrily.

"Your diamond?" Doc said. "Why, that's the diamond *I* found for Snow White!"

They looked at each other.

"Dopey! Dopey!" they yelled frantically and ran toward him.

Dopey looked up and his hammer fell onto the diamond. It broke into two pieces! All of the other Dwarfs were upset. But Dopey realized something they didn't.

At the mine's entrance, the end-of-the-day whistle blew.

"It can't be that late already!" cried Doc. "What will we do? Snow White will be waiting for us when we get home!"

"So will the Prince," Grumpy said.

Doc sighed. "We'll just have to explain."

At the Dwarfs' cottage, Snow White had been busy cooking all day. She had just set the table when the Prince arrived.

"Hello," Snow White said with a smile. "My gift should be here soon. Then we'll eat dinner."

"That sounds wonderful, darling!" the Prince exclaimed.

Just then, the Dwarfs arrived. Doc carefully set a bag with his diamond in front of Snow White, while Grumpy gave his to the Prince.

Snow White and the Prince looked at each other in surprise.

The Prince picked up his bag. "We must think alike," he said. "This is my present for you. It's for your crown. Grumpy helped me find it."

Grumpy crumpled his cap and looked down at his shoes. He wished that he'd found a better gift for the princess.

"Oh, darling," Snow White said to the Prince as she held up the broken diamond. "How unusual!"

"Yes," said the Prince, disappointed. "Unusual."

"And I have something for you." Snow White beamed as she handed the Prince her bag.

The Prince opened the bag and pulled out the other part of the diamond.

"Oh, my!" said Snow White in surprise.

The Prince squeezed Snow White's hand. "It's beautiful, my dear, because it is from you," he said.

Dopey came over to the table and pointed to Snow White's diamond and the Prince's diamond.

"Yes, they are beautiful, Dopey," said Snow White. She patted his arm.

Dopey shook his head and pointed to each of the pieces again.

"I'm sorry." said the Prince. "I don't understand, Dopey."

As the Prince and Snow White watched, Dopey joined the two separate pieces together.

"Oh, look!" Snow White exclaimed. "It's a heart! The diamonds are just like us—two halves that are perfect together!"

"You're right!" the Prince exclaimed.

266

The next night at the anniversary ball, Snow White and the Prince danced happily while the diamond heart sparkled nearby. It would always remind the prince and princess of their wonderful first anniversary.

Ariel & Melody

When Ariel, the little mermaid, married Eric, she became a human so that she and Eric could live together at the palace. Eventually, Ariel had a baby girl. She was named Princess Melody, and Ariel and Eric were both very happy.

One day, Ariel's father, King Triton, came to the surface to see his new granddaughter. He had a special present for her: an enchanted necklace. "My precious Melody," Triton said, "this is so you will never forget that a part of your heart will always belong to the sea." He opened the locket, and a beautiful vision of the underwater world of Atlantica appeared.

As Triton was about to place the necklace around his granddaughter's neck, a giant black tentacle splashed out of the water and snatched Melody from Ariel's arms! The tentacle belonged to the evil sea witch Morgana.

Like her sister, Ursula, Morgana wanted to control the seas—but to do that, she needed the king's powerful trident. The witch climbed into the ship and called to her ferocious pet—a tiger shark named Undertow—to swim next to them.

"Hand over the trident," she ordered King Triton as she dangled the baby over Undertow's open jaw, "or your precious granddaughter will be shark chow!"

Just as Triton was about to give up his trident, Ariel sprang into action. She cut a sail rope, and a heavy beam slammed against Morgana and knocked her into the water. Melody flew from the sea witch's tentacle. Eric grabbed onto a rope and swung out over the water to catch her.

With a blast from his trident, King Triton shrank Undertow into a guppy, but Morgana managed to escape. "Find her!" Triton shouted to his men.

Days later, there was still no sign of Morgana.

Ariel handed the enchanted necklace to Triton. "Until Morgana is found, Melody can't go into the sea. She can't know about merpeople or Atlantica . . . or even you, Daddy."

Triton sadly agreed. He dropped the necklace into the ocean, and then returned to his underwater kingdom.

Over time, Melody grew into a beautiful young princess. Her parents built a wall to keep her away from the sea, but that didn't stop her. She liked to swim among the colorful fish and collect seashells and rocks from the ocean floor. Her guardian, Sebastian the crab, had a hard time keeping up with her!

On her twelfth birthday, Melody found the enchanted locket that Triton had dropped so long ago.

Later that night, Melody examined the mysterious necklace. "My name is on here!" she told her mother.

"Where did you get this?" Ariel asked, shocked. "Melody, you know you're not allowed in the sea."

"Why does this necklace have my name on it?" Melody asked. But Ariel wouldn't answer.

"You're hiding something from me!" Melody cried. Clutching the necklace, she ran to the ocean and climbed into a small boat.

Sebastian scurried after the young princess. "This necklace means something," Melody said to the crab. "If no one's going to tell me, I'm going to find out for myself!"

Deep in her cave, Morgana found out that Melody had run away. She sent Undertow to bring the girl to her.

When Melody arrived, the evil sea witch told her she was destined to be a mermaid. With a drop of magic potion, Morgana turned the girl into one. She promised to let Melody stay that way—in return for King Triton's magic

 trident. "It was stolen from me years ago," Morgana lied.

Melody swam off in search of the trident.

When Ariel found out that her daughter was missing, she and Eric went to look for her. King Triton appeared and changed Ariel back into a mermaid so she could search the seas. Eric would keep watch from his ship.

Meanwhile, Melody made her way to Atlantica and stole the trident from King Triton's throne room. While she was there, she unknowingly dropped her necklace.

Moments later, Triton and Ariel entered the throne room. They discovered that the trident was missing—and found Melody's locket!

With her friend Flounder, Ariel managed to find her way to Morgana's ice cave. They arrived just as Melody was about to hand Morgana the trident.

"Melody, don't!" shouted Ariel.

The little princess stared at her mother's tail.

"You're a mermaid!" she exclaimed.

"All this time and you never

told me?"

"She's lied to you all these years," Morgana said.

"Melody, if there was one thing I could do over—" Ariel started to say.

But Melody turned away. "Too late, Mom." She handed the trident to Morgana.

The sea witch cackled, grabbing the trident. "Your mummy was only trying to protect you from me!"

"You tricked me!" cried Melody.

"You have no one to blame but yourself!" Morgana hissed. "Oh, and by the way, your time as a mermaid has just about expired."

As Morgana used the trident, her power grew and grew. The merpeople fell under her spell.

"Bow down before me!" Morgana shrieked.

But since Melody was human again, the witch had no power over her. The girl grabbed the trident from Morgana and threw it to her grandfather. "I think this belongs to you!" she called to him.

King Triton blasted Morgana with the trident. "Never again will you threaten my family!" he thundered. A block of ice formed around Morgana and she fell deep into the sea.

Back on shore, Melody hugged her parents.

"Oh, Melody, I was so afraid we'd lost you," Eric said.

"I'm sorry," she said.

"We should have told you the truth," Ariel replied.

"I didn't mean to hurt anyone," Melody said. "I just hoped I'd be a better mermaid than a girl."

Ariel smiled. "Melody, sweetie, it doesn't matter if you have fins or feet. We love you for who you are on the inside."

Just then, Triton joined them. "Melody, I don't blame you for wanting to join us merfolk. And because you're my granddaughter, I'm giving you a most precious choice: mermaid or human. It's up to you."

Melody thought about it. How could she choose? Then she smiled. "I have a better idea."

Back home, Melody pointed the trident at the sea wall around the castle. *Boom!* The trident blasted a hole in the wall, and water rushed in.

The merpeople and Melody's friends from the sea swam to the palace steps. Melody dove into the water, happier than ever. Now she could truly be part of both worlds.

The Magic of True Love

Once upon a time, there lived a kindhearted girl named Cinderella. Lady Tremaine, her cruel stepmother, and Anastasia and Drizella, her two spoiled stepsisters, forced her to do all the cooking, cleaning, and other housework.

One fateful night, everything changed. With a little help from her Fairy Godmother, Cinderella was able to attend the royal ball, where she met and fell in love with the Prince.

Soon the couple married, and Cinderella and the Prince spent all of their time together. Their lives were happier than they had ever imagined they could be.

Cinderella's stepmother and stepsisters were not happy, though.
Since Cinderella wasn't around, they had to do all the chores!
Anastasia and Drizella hated washing dishes and scrubbing floors,
and they were constantly fighting with each other.

One day, Anastasia saw Cinderella and the Prince in the distance, and she followed the couple into the woods. Cinderella's Fairy Godmother had surprised them with an anniversary party.

Anastasia watched as the Fairy Godmother pointed her wand at Cinderella and the Prince and said, "Bibbidi-Bobbidi-Boo!" Suddenly, the royal couple was wearing the clothes they had worn on the night they met.

"So that's how Cinderella did it!" exclaimed Anastasia. "Magic!" She was still jealous of her stepsister.

As the Fairy Godmother sang to them, the Prince took Cinderella in his arms and danced with her in the moonlight. At the song's big finale, the Fairy Godmother got so excited that she threw up her arms, and her wand flew through the air. It landed right in front of Anastasia!

"Perfect!" Anastasia exclaimed. She snatched the wand and ran away.

As soon as she got home, Anastasia showed the wand to her mother and sister and told them the magic words.

Lady Tremaine was fascinated. "Do you know what this means, girls?" she said. "Power, riches, revenge!" She picked up the wand. "I call upon all the forces of the universe," she continued. "Bibbidi-Bobbidi-Boo! Reverse the moon and sun, turn back tide and time, unravel Cinderella's happily-ever-after to the moment my troubles began!"

Suddenly, the clock turned back a year. It was the exact moment that the Grand Duke had arrived with the glass slipper Cinderella had left at the ball.

Lady Tremaine and her daughters welcomed the Grand Duke into the sitting room. They knew that whoever's foot fit into the slipper would marry the Prince. Using the magic wand, Lady Tremaine secretly stretched the glass slipper to fit Anastasia's rather large foot. The Grand Duke declared that the Prince's bride-to-be had been found.

Cinderella watched the whole thing from upstairs. She was confused. "I danced with the Prince. That was my slipper," she told her stepmother. She pulled the matching glass slipper from her pocket.

Her stepmother snatched the slipper and dropped it, shattering it into many pieces. "Whatever you think happened last night was a dream," she said and left for the palace with Anastasia.

Jaq and Gus, Cinderella's two mouse friends, tried to comfort her. "Maybe just a big mistake," suggested Jaq.

Suddenly, Cinderella felt better. "Of course! A mistake! If I see him again, everything will be all right."

With her friends tucked safely in her pocket, Cinderella set out for the palace. Once there, she was able to get past the guards by pretending she was a servant.

When Cinderella finally found the Prince, he didn't remember her at all. He told her he was going to marry Anastasia that very night. Cinderella was heartbroken.

Luckily, Jaq and Gus discovered the truth: the wicked stepmother had put a spell on the Prince to make him fall in love with Anastasia.

"She made him forget who I am," Cinderella said to her mouse friends. "We have to get that wand!"

Cinderella watched through a keyhole as her stepsisters and stepmother locked the wand in a dresser drawer. Jaq and Gus would have to retrieve it!

The mice got the wand, but unfortunately, Lucifer the cat began to chase them.

"The wand!" Lady Tremaine cried.

"Mice!" screamed Anastasia.

The mice darted out the door and tossed the wand to Cinderella.

Soon the trio found the Prince. Cinderella pointed the wand at him, but before she could finish undoing the spell, the guards appeared. Lady Tremaine had told them Cinderella was a thief.

"I am not a thief!" Cinderella insisted. She turned to the Prince. "You're under a spell. That's why you don't remember me." She reached for him and their hands touched. Instantly, the Prince felt a connection.

"The poor child," Lady Tremaine said. "Obviously out of her mind."

Confused, the Prince soon left. Lady Tremaine turned to the guards. "Put her on the next ship leaving the kingdom. I want her banished forever," she ordered.

The guards obeyed.

After Cinderella had been led away, Jaq and Gus showed the Prince the other glass slipper, which the bluebirds had glued back together. They told him that he had been under a spell and his true love was on a ship that was about to sail away.

The Prince raced out the door. Once he and Cinderella were reunited on the ship, the spell was broken. Without hesitation, the Prince asked for Cinderella's hand in marriage. She happily agreed.

When the couple arrived at the palace, the Prince ordered the guards to arrest Anastasia, Drizella, and their mother. But they were nowhere to be found. They had used the magic wand to make themselves vanish.

That evening, as Cinderella prepared for her wedding, her stepmother appeared.

"How lovely you look," Lady Tremaine said. "It appears you were right, Cinderella. The Prince *does* want to marry you, and marry you he shall."

Then she summoned Anastasia. The sinister stepmother had used the wand to change her so she looked exactly like Cinderella. They were going to trick the Prince into marrying Anastasia!

Cinderella was horrified. But her stepmother didn't care. She pointed the wand at Cinderella and the mice. Magic sparkles surrounded them, and then—*poof!*—they were gone!

A moment later, Cinderella and the mice reappeared in a pumpkin coach. Lucifer had been changed into an evil coachman, whose job it was to get rid of Cinderella once and for all.

Cinderella grabbed hold of the vine that formed Lucifer's seat and pulled it hard enough to send him flying off the coach. *Splat!* He landed in a muddy stream and turned back into a cat. Jaq and Gus detached the horse's harness. Then Cinderella scooped up the mice and jumped onto the horse's back. She grabbed the reins and stopped the galloping horse right at the edge of a cliff. They were safe!

"Now what are we going to do?" asked Jaq.

"Well, I'm not going to miss my own wedding!" Cinderella declared. They rode toward the palace as quickly as they could.

Inside the palace, the wedding ceremony was already underway. "Do you, Cinderella, take this man as your lawfully wedded husband?" the bishop asked.

But Anastasia was having second thoughts. She wanted to marry someone who loved her for who she really was, not who she was pretending to be. "I . . . I . . . don't."

Just then, the real Cinderella ran down the aisle. Everyone gasped. There were two Cinderellas! Lady Tremaine and Drizella appeared. They looked very upset.

"You little ingrate!" the wicked stepmother hissed at her daughter. She aimed the magic wand at both Cinderella and Anastasia. "Bibbidi-Bobbidi-Boo!"

"No!" exclaimed the Prince. He pulled out his sword to protect Cinderella and Anastasia. The spell from the wand reflected off the sword and hit Lady Tremaine and Drizella instead!

Zap! They were turned into toads!